Attack of
the Blobs

Tony Bradman ◆ Jonatronix

Max's mission log

We are travelling through space on board the micro-ship Excelsa with our new friends, Nok and Seven.

We're on a mission to save Planet Exis (Nok's home planet), which is running out of power. The only way to do this is to collect the fragments that form the Core of Exis – the most powerful energy source in the galaxy.

So far we have collected four fragments, but we need to find a fifth! Only the king and queen of Exis (Nok's parents) know where the final fragment is hidden, so our next task is to find them. It's not easy. A space villain called Badlaw wants the power of the Core for himself.

Fragments collected so far: 4

In our last adventure ...

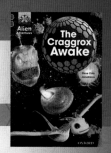

We were on our way to Planet Spongemar, following a clue that the king and queen had left, when we heard strange singing. It was coming from Sirens – dragon-like creatures that live in the depths of space.

The singing made us very sleepy. At first we thought the Sirens wanted us to crash in an asteroid field, but then we realized they were trying to help us steer away from it. The asteroids were living space rocks called Craggrox!

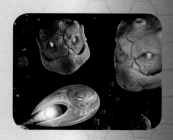

With the Sirens' help, we managed to get clear of the Craggrox. We're hoping to catch up with the king and queen on Planet Spongemar.

Chapter 1 – A nasty cold

Cat was in the sick bay on the micro-ship Excelsa. She couldn't stop shivering, but her head was burning hot. Lying in the body scanner, she watched Seven flick between screens on the monitor.

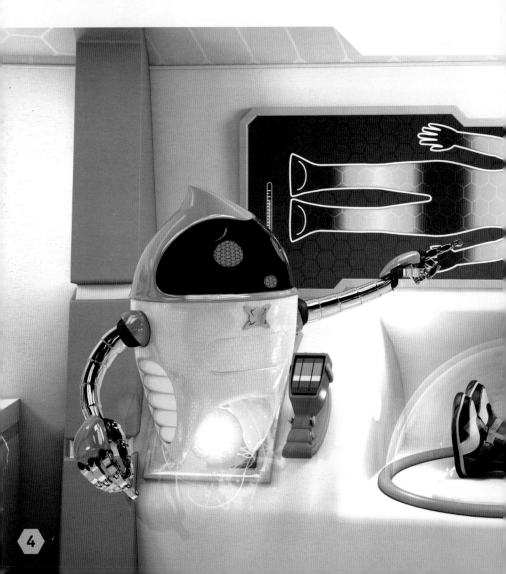

"Hurry up, Seven," Cat said impatiently. "I've got to get back to the bridge!"

Seven switched off the monitor. "You're not going anywhere," he said. "You have a very bad cold."

"I have to go!" Cat argued. "I'm supposed to be navigating to Planet Spongemar ..." She began to cough.

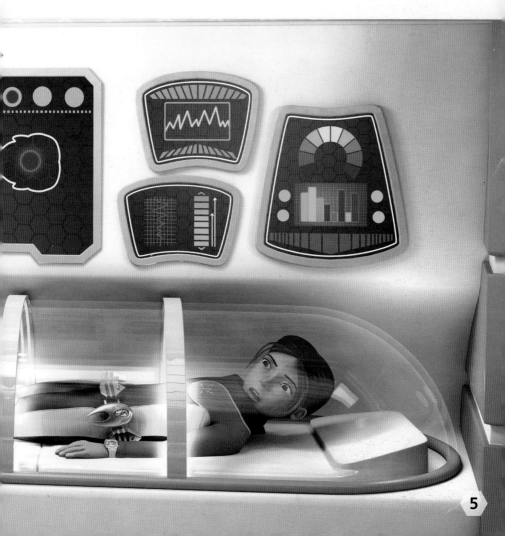

As Cat sat up she caught a glimpse of her reflection. Her nose was red and her eyes looked puffy.

"Why do I feel so dizzy?" she groaned.

"Your body is trying to fight off a cold. It has to make things called antibodies to fight the germs," replied Seven. "Don't worry. You'll soon get better with lots of rest."

Seven got a brightly-coloured bottle of medicine from the cabinet. He poured some into a glass and handed it to Cat. "Drink this," he said. "It will make you feel better."

Cat looked at the glass. A thick, yellow liquid fizzed in the bottom. She took a sip. "Yuck!" Cat spluttered. "It tastes like cold gravy!"

Cat tried to get up. "I need to navigate ..."

"Don't worry, Tiger is taking care of the navigation," Seven replied.

"Tiger!" Cat said, coughing hard. "He's bound to get us lost! I'm fine now. That medicine has done the trick!" She gave another loud sneeze.

"I'm sure Tiger can manage," said Seven.

Chapter 2 – Curious footprints

On the bridge, Tiger was pointing excitedly at the viewscreen. There was a large, yellow planet up ahead. It looked like a giant, squashy bath sponge.

"Planet Spongemar! Good work, Tiger. You got us straight here," said Max. "Take us down, Nok."

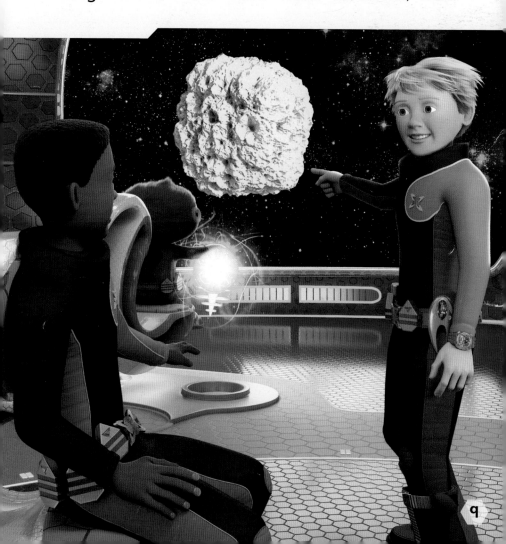

As they skimmed over the planet's surface, Nok watched the viewscreen hopefully. "There's no sign of my parents."

"It doesn't mean they're not here," Max said. "We'll search everywhere, I promise."

Nok brought the Excelsa gently in to land on a flat piece of ground.

As they touched down, Cat appeared on the bridge looking pale and shaky.

"I'm coming with you," she said.

Max glanced at Seven who was hovering behind Cat, shaking his head.

"I need you and Seven to stay here and look after the ship," said Max.

Grumpily, Cat flopped down on to her chair.

The air outside the ship was damp and smelled of rotten eggs.

Tiger coughed. "Phew! It stinks!"

"Helmets on, everyone," said Max.

They did as Max instructed. Then they all grew to normal size. The planet's spongy, yellow surface stretched as far as they could see.

"Let's make for those hills," said Nok. "My parents might be sheltering there."

Every step was hard work as their feet sank into the planet's moist surface.

Ant noticed that they were leaving deep footprints in the ground. "*Interesting*," he said to himself.

Tiger stopped, exhausted. "Let's use our holo-boards," he suggested.

"Good thinking," replied Max.

The holo-boards worked for a while, but then they began to splutter and fade.

"I don't think the holo-boards like the dampness," Ant pointed out.

"Let's land and split up," said Max. "We can cover more ground that way."

Max and Tiger set off, tramping over the spongy landscape.

Ant and Nok were about to set off too, when Ant spotted something on the ground.

"Wait, look at this!" he said.

Angry red blisters were growing inside their footprints.

Nok wasn't listening. "Come on, Ant," he said, hurrying off up the hill. "There's no time to waste. We need to find Mum and Dad."

Chapter 3 – Sticky goo

Fascinated, Ant stared at the footprints for a few moments longer. As he did so, the blisters bubbled up into bigger red blobs ... and kept growing!

"Nok! Come back!" Ant called, but his friend was too far ahead to hear him.

Suddenly a cry echoed round the hills. "Help!"
It was Nok.

"I'm coming!" Ant shouted.

Ant bounded up the hill as fast as he could.
He found Nok trapped by sticky, red blobs that
were spreading over his feet.

"Hold my hand," said Ant urgently.

Nok grabbed on and Ant activated his power boots. Then Ant blasted high into the air, pulling Nok free. They landed on a clear patch of land.

Nok breathed a sigh of relief. "Thanks, Ant!" said Nok.

"Look!" said Ant, pointing at the hill.

Nok followed Ant's gaze and saw a six-sided symbol imprinted on the soft surface. Inside the hexagon was a cone shape.

"It's another clue, Nok!" said Ant.

"Yes," said Nok sadly, "but that means my parents are no longer here on Planet Spongemar."

"At least we know they've been here," replied Ant, taking a photo of the clue with his watch.

"Planet Gakarak is cone-shaped," said Nok, looking at the clue again. "Maybe they've gone there."

"Great! We can run it through the computer when we get back to the ship to make sure," said Ant excitedly.

Max and Tiger appeared from round the other side of the hill.

"We heard you calling for help, Nok," Max said. "What's happened?"

Ant quickly explained about the blobs. "We're not safe. We should get moving in case we get stuck again."

"They're only red blobs," said Tiger. "They can't be that dangerous."

Tiger reached down and picked up one of the blobs. He held it up. A thick, red goo oozed down his sleeve.

"Ugh, this is disgusting!" said Tiger.

Suddenly his spacesuit fizzed and a curl of smoke appeared from a hole in his sleeve.

"It's burning through my suit!" cried Tiger, dropping the blob.

"It's like acid!" said Max. "We need to get back to the ship without any of the blobs touching us."

The friends charged down the hill as the blobs bubbled up behind them.

Chapter 4 – The blobs multiply!

At the bottom of the hill, Ant looked over his shoulder. "There are more blobs, and they're getting bigger!" he said.

Tiger looked back. Some of the blobs were growing to an enormous size. Worst of all ... they were on the move!

The giant blobs rolled quickly towards the four friends.

"Faster!" cried Max.

The friends ran back towards the ship. More blobs kept on emerging out of the ground around them.

The friends followed Max as he weaved through the blobs. Sticky goo was now dribbling all over the ground, making it harder to move.

"We're not going to make it!" yelled Tiger. "There are too many of them."

"It's not far to the ship now," Max reassured him. "I'm sure we'll get there ..."

"I don't know about that," cried Ant. "Watch out, everyone!"

Right in front of them, a huge blob pushed up through the ground ... and this one had teeth!

The enormous blob monster loomed over the boys. They all froze.

Then it lunged at them. Its jelly-like body stretched forwards as it snapped its huge teeth. Ant and Nok only just sprang out of the way in time.

"Quick, everybody. Shrink!" cried Max. "Smaller targets will be harder for it to find."

They shrank and the monster blob rolled to a halt. It turned this way and that in confusion.

"It'll be even harder to get back to the ship while we're this size," moaned Tiger. The ground was sticky with goo. "We'll never make it."

Max pushed the button on his suit. "Use your wings."

The friends began to fly back towards the Excelsa. The blobs seemed to sense their rapid movement as hundreds of the red monsters started rolling after them.

"Hurry!" cried Max.

As the Excelsa finally came into view, Nok cried out in horror. Red blobs covered almost the entire surface of the ship. Goo oozed from them and ran in sticky streams on to the ground.

"How are we going to reach Cat and Seven?" asked Ant.

"I don't know," said Max, as he stared helplessly at the Excelsa.

Chapter 5 – Close escape

As the micro-friends flew towards the Excelsa, three enormous blob monsters rose out of the ground. They were even more terrifying than the last ones, as they had large pincers that snapped at the air in front of the children.

At that moment there was a grinding noise from the Excelsa. The escape hatch at the front of the ship opened.

Cat stood in the doorway. "Hurry!" she called, beckoning towards her friends.

Dodging the monsters' snapping pincers and gnashing teeth, Max, Ant, Tiger and Nok flew towards the Excelsa.

Finally, they reached the hatch. Ant landed on the deck of the ship first and ran inside. Nok was close behind him, followed by Max.

Tiger was just coming in to land when, at the last moment, one of the monster's pincers caught his holo-wing.

"Help!" he cried.

Without thinking, Max launched himself towards the blob monster. He blasted the pincer with his power boots. The creature dropped Tiger, and Cat dragged him to safety.

"I see you've got your strength back, Cat," said Tiger breathlessly. "Thanks!"

"No problem! Seven's medicine has made me feel much better."

"Come on, let's ... *Atishoo!*" Max sneezed. Seven passed him a tissue. "Oh, no, I think I've caught your cold, Cat."

Max was still sneezing as they got back to the bridge.

All of a sudden the planet shook as though there was an earthquake and a burst of goo hit the viewscreen.

"It sounds as though the planet is sneezing, too!" joked Tiger.

Seven looked at Max, then back at the viewscreen.

"You're right, Tiger!" Seven said. "The planet *is* sneezing."

"What are you talking about?" asked Cat.

"I think this planet is a living creature," explained Seven. "It is reacting to us as though we're germs. The blobs are its antibodies. It's using them to fight us off."

Planet Spongemar

Planet Spongemar is a giant, living sponge. It is the only one of its kind. It is highly sensitive and reacts badly if any aliens land on it. Nothing can survive on Spongemar for long.

Known life forms
▶ The whole planet is alive.

Surface conditions
▶ Damp and drizzly
▶ Spongy soft ground

spongy yellow surface ●●○○○○○

hills ●●●○○○○○○

Spongebodies

Planet Spongemar makes its own version of antibodies – spongebodies – to defeat intruders. The spongebodies become more aggressive the longer the intruders stay. The advice is: don't travel to Spongemar.

Chapter 6 – The big sneeze

"Now we know what this planet is, let's get out of here," said Nok.

"Yes, I think that would be best for us *and* for the planet," said Seven.

"Let's see if we can shake off these antibodies," said Max. "Prepare for blast-off!"

They all took their places and Tiger fired up the engines. The ship started to rise, but the sticky antibodies rose up around the ship and pulled it back again ... *THUMP!*

"We're stuck!" said Ant. "The blobs are pulling us down!"

"There must be *something* we can do!" said Tiger.

"I've got an idea," said Cat.

43

"Seven, have you got any more of that medicine you gave me?" asked Cat. "A lot more?"

"I can make as much as we need in the fabricator," said Seven. The fabricator was a machine that could make anything it was programmed to. "Are you feeling unwell again?"

"It's not for me," said Cat. "It's for the planet!"

While Seven made the medicine, Cat explained her plan. The medicine would make the planet feel better, so the blobs and goo would disappear – just like it made her cold disappear. Once the blobs were gone, the Excelsa would be free and they could escape.

A few minutes later, Seven began pumping medicine out of the ship on to the surface of the planet. The red blobs started to disappear and the goo began to dry up.

"It's working!" said Ant.

There was a rumble outside and the ship began to shake.

"What's happening now?" asked Tiger.

"I think we're about to find out," said Max. "Brace yourselves, everybody!"

The shaking stopped for a brief instant. Then, a massive explosion blasted the Excelsa into the air.

"A...TISHOO!"

The micro-ship was sneezed off the planet.

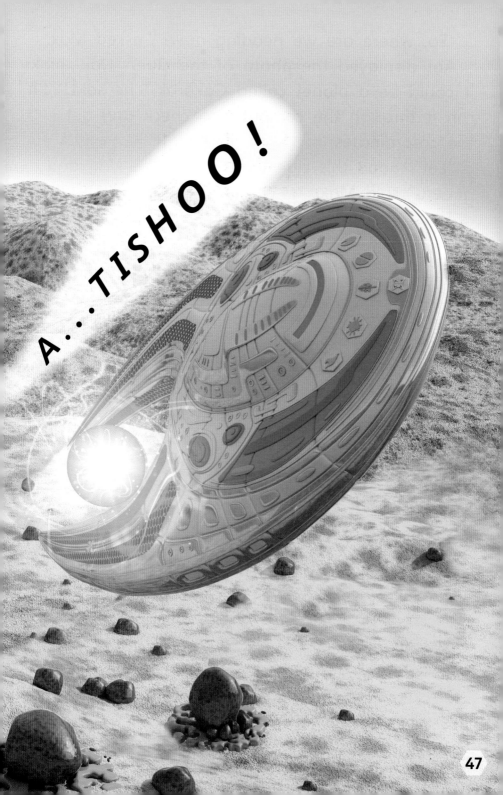

"So, where are we heading now?" asked Max.

Ant displayed the photo of the clue. "Nok thinks it could be a planet called Gakarak," he said. "I'll run it through the computer to check and get the co-ordinates."

"Let's hope this clue leads us to the king and queen," said Max.

Time was running out.

Find out what happens next in *The Image Maker.*